THE HARDY BOYS®

SECRET FILES #1

~~ Trouble at the Arcade ~~

MONEY BOX

BY **FRANKLIN W. DIXON**

ILLUSTRATED BY **SCOTT BURROUGHS**

SCHOLASTIC INC.
New York Toronto London Auckland
Sydney Mexico City New Delhi Hong Kong

ISBN 978-0-545-24851-8

Text copyright © 2010 by Simon & Schuster, Inc.
Illustrations copyright © 2010 by Scott Burroughs. All rights reserved.
Published by Scholastic Inc., 557 Broadway, New York, NY 10012, by arrangement with Aladdin, an imprint of Simon & Schuster Children's Publishing Division. THE HARDY BOYS is a registered trademark of Simon & Schuster, Inc. SCHOLASTIC and associated logos are trademarks and/or registered trademarks of Scholastic Inc.

12 11 10 9 8 7 6 5 4 3 2   10 11 12 13 14 15/0

Printed in the U.S.A.   40

First Scholastic printing, January 2010

Designed by Lisa Vega
The text of this book was set in Garamond.

CONTENTS

1

Alien Attack!

All humans will be destroyed!" a metallic voice rang out.

Nine-year-old Frank Hardy gasped as yet another row of hideous aliens appeared over the horizon. There was no question about it. Earth was being invaded!

"Ha!" he shouted, and his dark hair fell in his eyes as he dodged a laser blast by doing a somersault through the air. Then he ducked around a huge pile of rocks.

Oh no! There were more aliens behind the rock pile. And these were even worse. They were spitting horrible blue goo!

BLURP! A wad of goo came flying at Frank.

He jumped up and did a flip in midair to avoid the goo. Then he karate-kicked a rock. It crashed down on one of the aliens.

SPLAT! Blue goo spurted everywhere.

"Gotcha!" Frank cried.

"Frank! Are you up there?"

For a second Frank thought one of the aliens was calling him. Then he realized it wasn't an alien. It was his mother. He blinked and looked up from the video game console.

BLURP! On the screen, the aliens were still coming. A few seconds later a big blob of goo took over the screen, and then two words appeared:

"Rats," Frank muttered. "I'll never be ready for the contest if I don't do better than that."

His mother called his name again. He set down the controls and walked out to the top of the stairs to see what she wanted.

"Oh, there you are." Mrs. Hardy was holding a large spoon in one hand and a book in the other. She was a librarian, and she almost always had a book with her. "It's Joe's turn to set the table for dinner," she said. "But I can't find him anywhere. Have you seen him?"

"Nope." Frank started down the stairs. "But don't worry. I'll find him."

He went out the back door and crossed the lawn, heading toward the woods at the back of the yard. Before he got there, he looked around carefully.

There were hedges on both sides of the yard, so none of the neighbors could see him. The sound of hammering was coming from the spare room over the garage. Mr. Hardy had been working up there for weeks during his free time. But Frank couldn't see his father through the window, so he guessed his father couldn't see him, either.

Frank ducked into a narrow path between two bushes. It looked like a trail that nothing but a deer or a rabbit would use. But it actually led straight to the tree house Frank and his younger brother Joe had helped their parents build in the woods. No one except the two of them (and their parents) knew the tree house was there.

The tree house was halfway up a huge old maple tree. Frank and Joe had painted the bottom of the platform green and brown. That way, even if someone walked right past, they probably wouldn't notice it.

At least not most of the time. Right now any-one passing by would definitely see it. That was because Joe had left the ladder hanging down.

The ladder was made out of rope and planks. It had a pulley system so the boys could keep it rolled up out of sight whether they were in the tree house or not.

Frank grabbed the ladder and started to climb. Soon he was peering into the tree house. It was one big room inside. The back wall was the trunk of the tree, and the front wall had the door and a window cut

out of it. One of the side walls was covered with posters from martial arts and monster movies, and the other had a dry-erase whiteboard where the brothers could leave notes for each other. There was no real furniture, but there were some cushions to make sitting on the floor more comfortable.

Eight-year-old Joe Hardy was sitting on one of the floor cushions, reading comic books. His dirty-blond hair was sticking up in one place like he hadn't brushed it when he'd gotten out of bed. "Hi," he said when Frank climbed in. "What's up?"

"You forgot to pull up the ladder," said Frank. "Are you crazy? We don't want Adam to find this place."

Adam Ackerman lived on the other side of the woods. He was in Frank's class at school and was known as the meanest bully in Bayport.

Joe just shrugged. "Well, he didn't find it, did he?"

Frank frowned. Joe was always saying stuff like that.

"Mom's looking for you," he said. "It's your turn to set the table."

"Okay." Joe tossed the comic book he was reading into the messy pile beside him. Then the two boys climbed back down the ladder and used the pulley to lift it back out of sight.

"What were you doing out here, anyway?" Frank asked as they pushed their way out of the woods. "You should be practicing for the video game tournament tomorrow. Otherwise you'll never make it past the first round."

That was why Frank had been playing Alien Blob Blaster. The tournament was being held at the grand reopening of the arcade at Bayport Fun World. The grand prize was a brand-new super-deluxe game system.

"Who needs practice when you have natural

talent?" Joe bragged. "I'm not only planning to make the finals—I'm planning to win!"

"Don't be so sure," said Frank. "That VidPoint 3000 game is way better than the one we have. Tons of people will be there trying to win it. That's why you need to practice. With both of us entering, we'll have twice the chance of winning."

"We?" Joe echoed with a grin. "Who says I'm going to share when I win that game?"

Frank rolled his eyes. "What choice do you have? We share a room, remember?"

"Maybe not for long." Joe looked toward the garage. The sound of hammering was still coming from that direction. "Dad's almost finished fixing up the spare room. And you know what that means!"

"No. What?"

"Duh!" said Joe. "It means we'll finally get our own bedrooms!"

Frank cast a dubious look at the garage. "I doubt it," he said. "The spare room is practically a whole separate apartment from the rest of the house. Mom and Dad aren't going to let either of us live out there."

"If you're so sure, I guess that means you don't mind if I'm the one who moves out there," Joe said. "Cool. You can keep our tiny old room. You can even have both bunk beds all to yourself. I'll just fill up all the space in my brand-new room with my brand-new VidPoint 3000."

"Dream on," Frank said. "I've been practicing all week for that contest. You'll be sorry you didn't want to share when *I* win that game system."

They were almost at the back door by now. Joe stopped and grinned at his brother. "If you're so sure you can beat me, why don't we make a bet?" he said. "Whichever one of us wins that contest gets to move into the spare room—with the 3000 all to himself."

Frank could tell that Joe was sure he was going to win. That made him kind of mad.

"You're on," he said. "It's a bet!"

2

Fun World

I'll probably get the highest score ever today," Joe bragged. He leaned forward as far as his seat belt would let him, trying to see out the front window of his father's car. He was eager to catch his first glimpse of Fun World. It was the day of the video game tournament, and he couldn't wait!

Frank was sitting beside him. "Don't count on it," he said. "I practiced all week. I'll probably break the world record."

"Only until I take my turn and beat your sorry score!" Joe shot back.

"All right, boys, that's enough." Fenton Hardy looked at them in the rearview mirror. "It's fine to want to do your best and win. But you don't have to insult each other."

"Sorry, Dad," said Frank.

Joe shrugged. "He started it."

Their father sighed. He'd just stopped at a red light, so he turned around to look at them this time. "What's gotten into you two?"

Joe shot Frank a warning look. Their parents didn't know about the boys' bet for the spare room. And Joe wanted to keep it that way. He was afraid Frank might spill his guts, though. He always wanted to tell adults everything.

But this time he kept quiet, and so did Joe. The light turned green, and Mr. Hardy drove on.

"Anyway, don't forget that you're brothers," he

said. "You're supposed to be a team. You'll always have a better chance if you work together instead of against each other."

"I guess," Frank said. He didn't sound too sure.

"It's just like my work with the police department," Mr. Hardy went on. "I have my strengths and skills, and so do they. That's why we all work as a team to stop criminals."

Mr. Hardy was a private investigator. He'd solved all kinds of crimes in Bayport and beyond, and he worked with the police a lot. Still, Joe didn't see what that had to do with him and Frank.

By now they were pulling into the Fun World parking lot. Mr. Hardy drove past the mini-golf course and batting cages and stopped in front of the entrance to the arcade.

"Here we are," he said. "Call when you need a ride home. Have fun, guys—and remember, you're a team!"

"Sure, Dad," Frank said. "Thanks for the ride."

The arcade entrance was a big glass door with a blinking sign over it. A skinny teenage boy was sitting by the table just inside. There was a rickety-looking wooden box beside him with cash in it, and also a huge roll of tickets. A door off to one side opened into a hallway that led to the main part of the arcade.

"Welcome to Fun World," the teenager said.

Joe recognized him. His name was Darryl, and his dad owned Fun World. The whole family lived just a couple of blocks from the Hardys. Darryl's dad called himself Mr. Fun, but his real name was Mr. Moore.

"Hi," said Frank. "We're here to enter the contest."

"You need to buy some of these." Darryl grabbed the roll of tickets. "You use them to play the games, and if you get a good enough score,

the machines give you more tickets back. You can trade the tickets for prizes or food inside, or just keep playing more games with them."

"Cool!" Joe said. "I'll take five dollars' worth." He pulled a five-dollar bill out of his pocket and tossed it into the cash box. "Of course, I probably won't need that many once I start racking up high scores."

"Sure," muttered Darryl, still sounding bored. "Here are your tickets."

The arcade was already crowded when Frank and Joe went in. It was divided into several huge rooms with archways in between. Signs pointed to the Prize Pavilion up front and the Snack Shack at the back. There were also signs about the tournament.

"The seven-to-nine age group is over there," Frank read. "That's us. Come on!"

They hurried over and got in line. A few people they knew were already there waiting.

"Hi, Hardys!" someone called. It was their friend Iola from school. "Look, Chet's taking his turn right now." She pointed to the Alien Blob Blaster game at the head of the line.

Chet Morton was Iola's brother. He was also

a good friend of both Hardy brothers. "Go, Chetster!" Joe yelled.

"Shh," warned Frank. "You'll distract him."

A moment later the game was over. Chet turned around with a big grin on his moon-shaped face.

"Yo!" he cried. "Beat that score, everyone!"

He was only joking. His score was terrible.

There was a teenage attendant keeping track of the scores. He looked much more cheerful than Darryl Moore. "Don't forget your prize tickets," he said. "Um, I mean ticket."

The machine had just spit out a single ticket. Chet shrugged and grabbed it. "One's better than none, right?" he joked.

Next a girl stepped up to the game. "Who's that?" Joe wondered.

"She's in my class," Frank said. "She's new. I forget her name."

Iola heard him and turned around again. "It's Callie," she said. "Her family just moved to Bayport. She's really nice."

Joe didn't care how nice the new girl was. He only cared about her score. When she finished her turn, a whole bunch of tickets spit out of the machine.

"Good going!" the attendant said after he checked the results. "You're in second place!"

"Congratulations," Frank said to Callie as she walked by.

"Thanks," she responded in a quiet voice.

"Yeah, pretty good job," said Joe. "But don't get too excited about it. I'm going to double your score!"

"Don't listen to him," Frank told her. "I'm the one who's going to win today."

Up ahead, Adam Ackerman was taking his place at the game. "Ugh," Joe whispered to Frank. "I didn't know he was here."

Adam was at the game for a long time. When he finally finished, he was grinning. "Beat that score!" he bragged.

Unlike Chet, he wasn't joking. Adam's score was really high.

The attendant looked at it. Then he checked his list. "Congratulations," he told Adam. "You have the high score of the day so far!"

3

A Major Score

Frank stared at Adam's name. The attendant had just written it in big letters at the top of the high-scores list.

"This stinks," Joe whispered. "It means rotten Adam will definitely be in the finals."

"I know." Frank watched as a whole line of tickets poured out of the machine. The higher your score, the more tickets you got. And Adam was getting a *lot* of tickets.

Adam smirked as he grabbed the tickets and

stuck them in his pocket. "Wow," he said loudly. "I hope I can figure out how to spend all these tickets! I'll probably have to buy out the whole prize counter!"

Chet wandered over to where the Hardys were standing. "Can you believe Adam's winning?" he whispered, looking nervous. Adam picked on him a lot. "This is going to make him brag even more than he already does."

"I know." Frank watched a kid from another school take his place at the machine. "I hope someone beats his score soon."

"Yeah," Joe agreed. "That'll wipe the stupid smile off his face."

But the next three or four people fell short. Each time the attendant announced the score, Adam looked even more smug.

Finally he yawned loudly. "This is getting boring," he announced. "I think I'll go trade a couple of my tickets for a soda. Call me when it's time for me to come back and win the finals."

Joe gritted his teeth. "We have to beat him!" he growled.

"We?" Frank echoed. "I thought we weren't working together."

"Hey, Iola's next," said Chet, elbowing Frank in the side. "She's awesome at this game. She always beats me."

"That's not saying much," Joe said with a grin.

Chet laughed. "I know," he admitted. "But she's really good. You'll see."

They all turned to watch. Chet was right. His sister *was* really good. But finally Iola got creamed by a purple blob monster in level six. That meant she was twenty points short of Adam's score.

"Great job. You're in second place," the attendant said. He wrote Iola's name on the high-scores list right below Adam's.

"At least she'll be in the finals," Chet said.

Frank nodded. "Maybe she'll beat Adam then."

"Chet! Iola! Where are you?" Mimi Morton yelled as she came running in. Mimi was Chet and Iola's four-year-old sister. She had a round face, blond hair, freckles like Chet, and bright green eyes like Iola.

"I didn't know Mimi was here," Joe said.

Chet looked guilty. "I sort of forgot she was," he admitted. "Iola and I are supposed to be watching her while Mom runs some errands at the shopping center across the street."

Mimi spotted Chet and skipped over. She always loved wearing bright colors and goofy outfits. But today she looked even weirder than usual. She had at least six beaded bracelets on each arm, seven or eight necklaces draped around her neck, and plastic rings on every finger. She even had several butterfly barrettes stuck in her wispy hair.

"Hey, Mimi, where'd you get all that stuff?" Iola asked, walking over to join them.

Mimi held out her arms to admire her bracelets. "A lady never gives away her fashion secrets," she said.

Joe rolled his eyes at Frank. Mimi was a pretty strange kid. She was always saying stuff like that. She liked to make up stories and pretend she was a princess or a movie star.

Chet poked her in the arm. "Come on," he said.

"There's no way you won enough tickets for all that stuff yourself. Where'd you get it?"

"I didn't win the tickets, I found them," Mimi said proudly.

"Found them?" Iola echoed. "Found them where?"

"On the floor." Mimi waved one arm around. That made her new bracelets jingle. "They were just lying there, so I picked them up."

Chet looked worried. "That's not right," he scolded her. "Someone probably dropped them and is looking for them. You should have turned them in at the front office."

"No way!" Mimi shook her head so hard her barrettes bounced. "I didn't want to go there. I don't like that mean boy."

"Mean boy?" said Frank. "You mean Darryl?"

"He chased me away before," Mimi said with a shudder. "All I wanted was some tickets!" She

26

giggled and started playing with one of her necklaces. "Lucky for me some tickets found me! They walked right up to me and jumped into my hand."

"Don't be dumb," said Chet, sounding annoyed.

Joe wasn't paying much attention to Mimi. "Hey, check it out," he said. "I'm up next." He rubbed his hands together and cracked his knuckles. "Prepare to be amazed!"

Chet and Iola laughed, but Frank shook his head. "Don't get too cocky," he told Joe. "That'll just make you more likely to mess up."

"Next!" the attendant called.

"Here I go," Joe said eagerly. He rushed over and stuck a ticket into the machine. Then he pressed the start button.

The alien blobs started coming. Joe took the controls and started blasting them. He was doing great.

"Take that, alien scum!" he yelled as he dropped

rocks on a whole row of aliens. Now he was at level two.

"Go, Joe!" Iola cheered. "Don't forget to watch out for the goo spitters."

Joe just nodded. He was totally focused on the

game. Soon he was at level three. Then level four. Level five . . .

"Attention, everyone!" a loud adult voice rang out. "May I have your attention, please! We have a very serious problem. The entrance money from the office is missing!"

4

Who's the Thief?

The announcement broke Joe's focus. He looked around and saw Mr. Fun, the owner of Fun World, standing in the middle of the arcade. He was frowning and looked very upset.

BLURP!

"Rats!" Joe exclaimed, looking back at the screen. An alien had just blobbed him. Game over.

"Good job," the attendant said. "You're in fourth place. You'll probably make the finals."

Joe didn't say anything. Fourth place wasn't good enough. He wanted to be first!

Tickets came spitting out of the machine. Joe took them and stuck them in his pocket.

Meanwhile, Frank was looking over at Mr. Fun. So were most of the other kids.

"What do you mean, the money is missing?" someone called out.

Mr. Fun didn't look like he was having much fun. His face was red and angry.

"I just went over to the office to collect today's entrance money," he said. "But it wasn't there!"

"What did Darryl say?" Frank called out. "Isn't he still in the office?"

Mr. Fun glanced at him. "He wasn't there. I guess he stepped away for a moment."

A boy from Joe's class shrugged. "If nobody was in the office, anyone could've come in off the street and grabbed the money."

"Yeah," Iola put in. "There wasn't even a lid on the box."

Mr. Fun shook his head. "Impossible," he said. "The front door was locked. Darryl knows better than to step away from the office without locking up." He glared around at all the kids. "It had to be someone inside Fun World who took the cash."

That made everyone start talking at once. Most of the kids in the arcade were gathered around by now. Joe saw Adam in the crowd, along with the new girl, Callie, and some other kids from school.

"Wow," Chet commented to the Hardys. "Too bad your dad isn't here. He'd be able to crack the case for sure."

"Yeah," Joe agreed. "Maybe we should call him."

"Wait, we should find out more first," Frank said. "What if that money just fell on the floor or something? Like Iola said, the box didn't have a lid. And when we came in, it was right on the corner of the table. Darryl might have knocked it off on his way to lock the door."

Joe raised his head. "Hey, Mr. Moore—I mean, Mr. Fun," he called out. "Did you check on the floor under the table?"

"Of course I did." Mr. Fun sounded kind of

annoyed. "That was the first place I looked. The cash wasn't there."

Some of the other kids started asking him questions. As Mr. Fun turned away to talk to them, Adam came swaggering over to the Hardys. He was staring at the list of top scores with a smirk on his face.

"Hey, Joe," he said. "Looks like you couldn't even come close to my incredible awesomeness. As usual."

Joe frowned. "That was only the qualifying round," he said. "I'm saving my best game for the finals."

"Yeah, right." Adam snorted. "With a score like that, you'll be lucky to even *make* the finals."

"Oh, shut up and drink your stupid soda," Joe snapped.

"What soda?" said Frank.

Joe realized that Adam wasn't holding any-

TOP QUALIFIERS
1. ADAM
2. IOLA
3. CALLIE
4. JOE

thing. "Oh," he said. "I thought he went to get a soda. What happened, Adam? Were you so obnoxious that someone poured it over your head?"

"Just keep making jokes, Hardy," Adam said with an even bigger smirk. "We'll see if you're still laughing when I totally destroy you in the finals and take home the prize."

Mr. Fun heard them. He looked over with a frown. "Don't get too excited about that, boys," he warned. "I'm shutting down the video game tournament until whoever took that money returns it. And if the cash isn't back within one hour, the contest is off for good!"

5

A Big Threat

"Shut down the tournament?" Joe exclaimed. "No way!"

"You can't do that!" someone else called out. "Most of us already did the first round!"

"Yeah," a third kid cried. "It's not fair!"

"Tell that to whoever took the money," said Mr. Fun. "As soon as I get it back, the contest's back on."

A bunch of other kids started muttering and staring at one another. Frank glanced over at

Adam. He expected Adam to be the most upset of all, since he was winning the contest so far. But Adam wasn't saying anything.

Iola noticed too. "Aren't you upset?" she challenged him. "Or are you not so sure you're going to win that video game system after all?"

Adam just shrugged. "Oh, I'm sure," he said. "But it's not a big deal."

At that moment Frank noticed a sudden movement at the edge of the crowd. He turned just in time to see someone disappearing through one of the archways. But the person was moving too fast for him to see more than a sneaker and a flash of blue jeans.

"Hey." Frank elbowed Joe. "Check it out. Someone just ran out of here at top speed!"

"Let's follow them," said Joe. "Maybe it's the thief!"

"Hey!" Chet called from behind them, sounding confused. "What's going on?"

"Come on," Iola said. "Let's go with them."

Frank glanced back and saw Iola and Chet running after them with Mimi trailing close behind. A few other kids were joining in the chase too, and even Mr. Fun was starting after them.

But he didn't have time to worry about them. Not if he and Joe wanted to catch up to whoever had just run away.

"I see someone!" Joe yelled, pointing ahead. "Up there! I think whoever it is just left the arcade."

Soon both Hardys were racing through the doorway leading into the rest of the Fun World complex. The first area they came to was the bumper cars arena. It wasn't very busy, but there were about five or six bumper cars out on the floor. Frank spotted a kid in jeans on the far side, heading for another door.

"Come on!" he shouted. "He's got a head start—we've got to catch up!"

"Let's take a shortcut," Joe said. He ran to the wall of the bumper car arena and vaulted over it.

Frank followed. The floor was pretty slippery, and when he landed he almost skidded out. But he caught himself and ran after Joe.

"Coming through!" Joe yelled as he ran.

A teenage boy was driving one of the bumper cars. When he saw the Hardys, his face lit up.

"Whoa!" he called to his friends in the other cars. "Let's get them!"

He aimed his car straight at Frank. "Hey!" Frank shouted. "Quit that!"

But the teenager just laughed. Frank had to jump aside to avoid the bumper car. It skidded past him and crashed into the wall. That made all the teenagers laugh.

Luckily, by then the brothers were both across. "Whew!" said Frank as he jumped over the other wall. "That was close."

Joe was staring ahead. "Through there," he panted. "Come on!"

They dashed through another doorway and found themselves in the Skee-Ball room. The long, narrow room was pretty

crowded. There were a lot of kindergartners running around, plus several adults pushing strollers. When Joe saw them all, he groaned.

"We'll never get through here!" he exclaimed.

Frank had just spotted a flash of blue up ahead on the far side of the crowd. He was pretty sure it was the kid they were chasing. But how were they going to catch up without knocking aside a bunch of little kids and babies?

Then he had an idea. "This way!" he yelled.

He led the way to the Skee-Ball lanes. They were like miniature bowling alleys, but raised up a foot or two off the ground. People were supposed to roll wooden balls up and into the holes at the top.

Frank jumped onto the end of the first lane. "Hey!" the kid playing there protested.

"Sorry!" Joe said as he followed Frank. "Just taking a shortcut."

They ran across the bottom part of all the lanes. Lots of people started yelling at them, but Frank tried to ignore them. Behind him, he heard a shout.

"Coming through! Pardon me, please!"

"That sounds like Mr. Fun," said Joe breathlessly as he ran.

Frank just nodded. He guessed that the owner must still be following them. "I just hope we can catch whoever it is in time," he said. "Otherwise, they could escape out another entrance."

Soon they reached the end of the line of Skee-Ball lanes. They had to leap over a trash bin at the far end. When he landed, Joe let out a shout.

"There!" he cried, pointing. "At the snack bar!"

Frank saw that Joe was right. The kid in blue jeans had run into the snack bar for this section of Fun World. It was in the back of the room, and there was no other exit. Joe put on a burst of speed and caught up to the other kid.

"Hey," he said in surprise as their quarry looked around desperately. "It's you. The new girl."

She turned around, her shoulders slumping. "Yeah," she said. "Hi. I'm Callie."

"We know." Frank had caught up by now. He stared at Callie. "Why'd you run away like that? Did you steal that money?"

"No way!" Callie said right away.

Frank could hear Mr. Fun and the others still coming. "Then why'd you run?" he asked.

Callie just shrugged and stared at the ground. A second later Mr. Fun and the others arrived. Chet and Iola were there, along with Adam and most of the others. Even Mimi was bringing up the rear.

Mr. Fun was huffing and puffing from the run. "Did you catch the thief, boys?" he asked.

"Um . . . ," Frank began uncertainly.

Suddenly Callie whirled around and pointed straight at Adam. "It was him!" she cried. "I saw him with that money. But when I told him he should give it back, he said he'd beat me up if I told anyone! That's why I ran away!"

6

A Real Mystery

What?" Mr. Fun roared, turning on Adam.

"No way!" Adam protested. "She's lying."

"No, I'm not." Callie folded her arms. "It was just a little while ago. I was at the other snack bar—the one in the arcade."

Mr. Fun nodded. "The Snack Shack."

"Adam was standing over by the counter," Callie went on. "He was counting a big stack of money—you know, dollar bills and stuff. But he stuck them in his pocket when he saw me looking."

"Oh yeah?" Adam challenged her. "Then how come there's no dollars in my pockets right now?"

He pulled both front pockets out of his pants. Joe leaned closer for a better look. All that came

THE SNACK SHACK

out of Adam's pockets were a few coins, a short paper clip chain, and a pebble. There was no sign of any paper money at all. Adam also turned around so everyone could see his back pockets. They were empty too.

Mr. Fun didn't look convinced. "I don't know," he said. "I think I'd better call your parents, young man."

"That's not fair!" Adam exclaimed. "The ones you should call are *her* parents." He pointed at Callie. "She's a liar!"

Callie's cheeks went pink. "I'm not a liar! You are!"

Mr. Fun looked uncertain. But before he could say anything, his son Darryl came jogging up.

"There you are, Dad," said Darryl, sounding annoyed. "I've been looking everywhere!"

Mr. Fun raised one eyebrow. "I could say the same to you," he said. "Where have you been?"

Joe's eyes widened when he saw that Darryl was holding a fistful of cash. "Is that the missing money?" he blurted out.

Darryl looked from Joe to the cash to his father. "Missing money?" he said. "What missing money?"

Mr. Fun looked stern. "Where did you get that cash, Darryl?" he demanded.

"It's mine," Darryl said with a frown. "This lady came in and asked if I'd help her carry some heavy stuff out to her car from one of the shops across the street. After I did, she gave me a tip." He waved the money he was holding.

Frank and Joe traded a look. Joe could guess what his brother was thinking. Was Darryl telling the truth? Or was that the money from the cash box?

"I locked the door while I was gone, just like you're always telling me to do," Darryl put in sullenly. "So what's the big deal?"

"The big deal is, the money from the cash box is gone!" his father snapped. "And I want to know where it went."

"Whoa." Now Darryl looked kind of worried. Suddenly he blinked. "Hey," he said, looking at someone behind his father. "Where'd *you* get all that stuff?"

Joe glanced that way and saw Mimi staring at Darryl. Her round cheeks started to turn pink, and she ducked behind Iola.

Darryl took a step toward her. "Why are you hiding?" he demanded. "Is it because you know you shouldn't have all those prizes?"

"Hey," said Frank. "Take it easy. She's just a little kid."

Darryl snorted. "I already chased her out of the office once earlier," he said. "She was sniffing around looking for extra tickets to trade for prizes." He narrowed his eyes as he glanced at

Mimi again. "I didn't give her any. So where'd she get all that loot? Maybe *she* stole that money, and some tickets, too."

Mimi burst into tears. "I didn't!" she sobbed, clinging to Iola. "A lady never steals stuff!"

Mr. Fun was starting to look confused and annoyed. "Come with me," he said, grabbing Darryl by the arm. "The rest of you, don't go anywhere. Especially you, you, and you." He pointed to Mimi, Callie, and Adam. Then he turned and dragged Darryl off toward the arcade.

Everyone else started talking and wandering after them. Iola and Chet were trying to stop Mimi from crying. Adam was glaring at Callie, who was ignoring him.

Frank shot Joe a look. "Wow," he whispered. "Now I really wish Dad was still here. This is turning into a real mystery!"

"Who needs Dad?" Joe whispered back with a grin. "We're eyewitnesses, right? I think we should try to solve the case ourselves!"

7

Who, What, When . . .

Frank hadn't thought about it that way. He realized Joe had a point. The two of them had been right nearby when the money got stolen, and they knew most of the people who might have done it. Plus, they knew all about solving crimes from listening to their father's work stories their whole lives. Who better to figure out the mystery than the two of them? Besides, it could be fun!

"Let's do it!" he agreed. "Dad's taught us a

lot about solving crimes over the years. So let's think about it—what would he do right now if he were us?"

"Give Adam a wedgie until he admits he took the cash?" Joe suggested.

Frank rolled his eyes. "No. He'd say that a good detective needs to figure out the *W*s."

"Huh?"

"Who, What, When, Where, Why, and How." Frank ticked each word off on his fingers.

Joe laughed. "Come on," he said. "Even I know 'How' doesn't start with a *W*."

"No, but it ends with one," said Frank. "I guess that counts. Anyway, Dad always puts it on the list."

Joe nodded. "Okay. So we already know What— the What is that someone took that money."

"Right," Frank said. "And we know Where. Right here at Fun World, in the office."

"Why's pretty easy too," Joe pointed out. "Everybody likes money."

"True. So all we need to do is figure out the rest. Especially the Who." Frank thought for a second. "I guess there are a few people who could be the Who. Let's go back to the arcade so we can keep an eye on them while we think about the other *W*s."

Soon the brothers were huddled behind a video game near the center of the arcade's main room. Adam was nearby, bragging about how he was going to win that contest if it ever started again. Callie was leaning against the wall by herself. Mimi had stopped crying after Chet traded in one of his tickets to buy her a lollipop.

"Okay, let's figure this out." Frank dug into his pockets. He found a scrap of paper and a stubby pencil and pulled them out. "We should start by making a list."

"Are you kidding?" Joe snorted. "Who needs

notes? This isn't school—it's a mystery! We should just go question people like Dad would do." He glanced around. "Starting with Adam Ackerman."

"Do you really think he could be the thief?" said Frank. "His pockets were empty—we all saw them."

Joe shrugged. "I still think he could've done it. He's always pulling rotten stuff at school, like stealing people's lunches."

"True," Frank agreed. "But when he steals a lunch, he can hide the evidence in his own stomach. I don't really think he ate that money."

Still, Frank wrote down Adam's name at the top of a list under the title "WHO?" Beside that he wrote down the other *W* words.

"Hmm," he said, staring at what he'd just written. "We know What, Where, and Why. We're trying to figure out Who and How. But what about When?"

"We know the crime must have happened between when we got here and when Mr. Fun announced that the money was missing," Joe said.

"That's not very specific," said Frank. "We were here for a while before he came out and said that. Maybe we should go ask Mr. Fun about when the cash actually disappeared."

They headed for the office. But when they got close to the door, they heard the sound of yelling.

"Yikes," Joe whispered. "Sounds like Mr. Fun's still yelling at Darryl."

"It's not my fault!" Darryl was yelling inside the office. "The stupid box was already half broken!"

Frank was still creeping closer. The door was standing partway open, and when he looked inside he gasped. "Look!" he exclaimed.

Joe came closer too. "Whoa!" he whispered.

Frank nodded. The wooden cash box they'd seen earlier wasn't on the table anymore. It was lying on the floor, smashed to smithereens!

8

A New Suspect

Check it out," Joe whispered. He kicked at a chunk of wood on the floor by his foot. "There are even pieces of that box way out here in the hall."

Frank nodded. "But why would someone bother to smash the box? It was wide open. All the thief had to do was grab the cash."

"Maybe the thief accidentally knocked over the box while he was running away," Joe guessed.

"It was pretty old, so it might have gotten smashed up just hitting the floor."

Just then there came the sound of stomping feet. A second later Darryl charged out through the door. He almost ran into the Hardys.

"Get out of my way!" he yelled. Then he stormed off down the hallway.

Joe peered into the office. Mr. Fun was sitting on the edge of the table.

"What is it?" he said when he saw the boys. "Did you come to tell me you found my money?"

"No," Joe said. "We were just wondering something. When exactly did you find out the money was missing?"

Mr. Fun frowned. "When do you think?" he snapped. "It was about two seconds before I started yelling that the money was missing!"

Joe glanced over at Frank. They could both

tell that Mr. Fun wasn't in a very good mood.

They ducked back out into the hall. "Should we go talk to Darryl?" Frank suggested. "Maybe he can tell us exactly when he left the office earlier."

Joe had a feeling Darryl was in just as bad a mood as his father. But he nodded. "Let's go find him."

That turned out to be harder than they

expected. Darryl wasn't anywhere in the arcade. But the Hardys finally spotted him in the bumper car arena. The other riders had left by now, and Darryl was the only one out on the floor. He was driving a bright purple bumper car around, smashing it into the parked cars as hard as he could.

"Hey, Darryl!" Joe called out. "Can we talk to you?"

Darryl didn't even look up. He just spun the purple car around and drove it straight toward the wall. It bounced off and crashed into another parked car.

"I guess he's not in a talkative mood," said Frank in a low voice. "Maybe we should wait."

"I have a better idea." There were two bumper cars parked along the wall right by where they were standing. Joe vaulted over the wall and jumped into one of them. "Come on!" he told Frank. "If we can catch up to him, maybe he'll talk to us."

Frank didn't look too sure. But he shrugged and jumped over into the other car.

Darryl looked over when he heard them coming. "Hey," he snapped. "This ride costs five tickets, you know. You can't just jump over the wall like that."

"We'll pay your dad back later," Frank said. "Right now we want to talk to you."

"I don't feel like talking. I feel like doing this." Darryl leaned over the steering wheel and drove straight toward

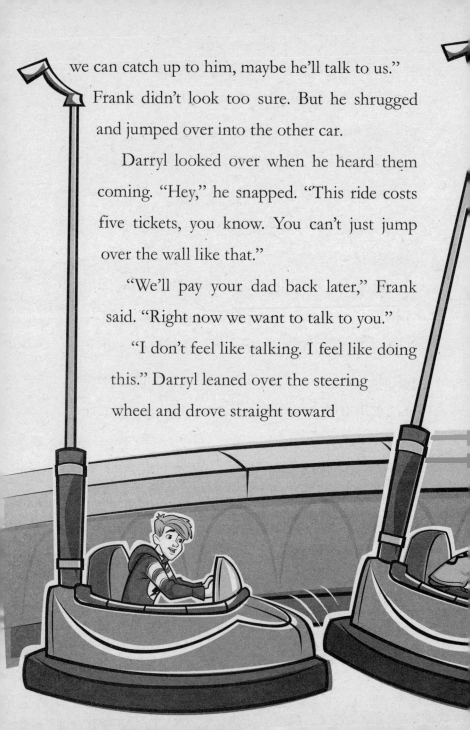

Frank's bumper car. Frank tried to steer away, but it was too late. Darryl's car crashed into his so hard that Frank's car jerked back and bumped into Joe's car.

"Whoa!" Joe cried.

Darryl's car bounced off the wall nearby. As soon as he could, he spun it around and took off for the opposite end of the arena.

Frank's car was stuck in the corner between a couple of parked cars. He was having trouble getting it turned around.

But Joe's car was still okay. "I'll go after

him!" he called. Then he stomped down on the go pedal. He steered after Darryl, dodging parked cars along the way.

He was almost caught up when Darryl heard him coming. "Leave me alone!" he yelled.

But Joe didn't slow down. He ran right into the back of Darryl's car. That made it bounce forward and get stuck between two parked cars along the wall.

"Hey!" Darryl shouted. He managed to spin his car around so it was facing out.

Joe didn't want to let him get away again. So he steered his car over to block the way.

"Get out of my way!" Darryl yelled. "Or I'll hit your stupid car so hard you'll end up on Mars!"

"I don't care." Joe clutched the steering wheel tightly, just in case. "I really need to ask you some questions."

By now Frank was steering toward them. "We're

just trying to help your dad get his money back," he called.

Darryl glared at both of them. For a second Joe thought he was going to follow through on his threat to ram them again.

But then the teenager slumped in his seat. "Whatever," he muttered. "My dad already thinks it's my fault the money is gone, and he won't listen to anything I say. So what do you want to know?"

"Well, to start with, what happened?" Frank asked.

"It was just like I said. That lady stopped in and offered me big bucks to help her carry some shopping bags out to her car, and I said yes. But, um, on the way out I might have knocked the cash box off the table."

"Might have?" Joe echoed.

Darryl glared at him. "Okay, I *did*," he said. "But it was an accident. I was so psyched to make that much cash for doing something so easy that I jumped up too fast. That stupid box was so old it smashed when it hit the floor."

Frank leaned forward on the steering wheel of his bumper car. "What happened to the money?"

"I didn't take it, if that's what you mean," Darryl said. "The money fell under the table. I was going to get it out from under there and clean up the box pieces as soon as I got back." He frowned, revving his bumper car. "But it took way longer than I thought to carry all that lady's stuff, and by the time I got back . . . Well, you know what happened."

"And you and your dad checked under the table, right?" asked Joe.

Darryl nodded. "The box was still there," he said. "And the roll of tickets, too. But not the money."

Joe was starting to feel impatient. "Come on," he said, swinging one leg over the edge of his car. "Let's go question some other people."

"Wait." Frank steered a little closer to Darryl's car. "We believe you didn't take the money. But we need more information so we can figure out who did. How long were you gone, exactly? And what time did you leave to help the lady?"

Darryl revved his car again. "What do I look like, a stopwatch?" he snapped. "If you want to know that stuff, you should ask that little brat with the blond braids. She was standing right there when the box broke."

"Huh?" Frank said. "Wait, do you mean Mimi?"

Darryl shrugged. "I don't know her name. She's been pestering me all day about tickets. She finally came back with a grubby dollar bill she wanted to use to buy some, but I didn't have time before I left."

Joe's eyes widened. He jumped the rest of the way out of his bumper car. "Aha!" he cried. "It was Mimi—she must have seen that money under the desk and taken it!"

9

Lost and Found

It didn't take long to find Mimi. She was in the arcade with Chet. The contest was still stopped, but a lot of kids were playing the different games. Chet was playing pinball while Mimi sucked on her lollipop nearby.

"Hi," said Chet when Frank and Joe raced up. "Where have you guys been?"

Joe didn't bother to answer. "Hey, Mimi," he said. "You didn't really find those tickets on the floor, did you? You found a bunch of money."

"Huh?" Chet looked confused. He turned away from his game. "What are you talking about?"

Mimi scrunched up her face. Her cheeks went red. "I might have found some money," she said. "But don't worry, I returned it to its rightful owner."

"What?" Chet squawked.

Frank leaned closer to Mimi. "What rightful owner?"

"I don't know his name." Mimi started playing with her bracelets. "He said he lost it. And then he gave me a big reward. I think he might be a secret prince or something."

"That's not what you said earlier, Mimi!" Chet exclaimed.

Frank and Joe traded a look. It was no surprise that Mimi's story had changed. She was always making things up and exaggerating. Usually it was harmless stuff, like pretending her dolls talked to her. Or that she was a princess. But this was different.

"So what did you do with the rest of the money?" Joe demanded. "Even all those prizes couldn't have used up more than a little of it."

Chet grabbed her by the arm. "Let's see in your pockets," he ordered his sister.

"Wait," Frank told them both. He'd just thought of something. "The Prize Pavilion doesn't take cash. Mimi had to use tickets to buy her prizes. And Darryl said he hadn't sold her any tickets."

"Duh!" said Mimi with a frown. "That was my reward, dummy. That secret prince guy gave me a whole bunch of tickets! Don't you know anything?"

She stomped away. Chet raced after her.

"Stop!" he called. "You're supposed to stay with me from now on, remember?"

The Hardys watched them go. "Do you think Mimi's telling the truth?" Frank asked.

"Who knows?" Joe said. "But if she is, it sounds like someone tricked her into giving him that money."

"It would have to be someone with a lot of tickets."

"Yeah. And you know who had access to lots of tickets?" Joe tapped his fingers on the pinball machine. "Darryl. Maybe he didn't get that cash from some mystery lady after all. Maybe he stole it himself!"

"Maybe." Frank wasn't too sure. "But if that's true, why would he walk right up to his father, waving the cash around? Besides, there are tons of other people here with plenty of tickets. Like Adam, for one."

"But if he took the money, where is it now?" Joe said. "His pockets were empty, remember?"

Frank nodded. That part was bothering him, too. "Maybe he hid the cash somewhere to pick up later."

Joe looked dubious. "I guess it's possible," he said. "Adam's always up to no good." He sighed. "I thought solving this crime would be easy. But it's not."

"Let's think about what Dad would do next," said Frank. He thought for a second. "He'd probably say to look for alibis."

"You mean figure out where everybody was at the time of the crime?"

"Yeah. That will help us figure out who *might* have done it and who *couldn't* have done it." Frank pulled out his list again and checked it. "For instance, Adam was at the Snack Shack getting a soda at the time."

"Except when he came back, he didn't have a soda," Joe recalled. "That seems kind of suspicious."

Frank tucked his list back in his pocket. "Definitely," he agreed. "Let's go check with the people at the Snack Shack and see if he was really there."

When the Hardys got to the Snack Shack, they found a college-age girl wiping the counter with a rag. Her name tag read SANDY.

"Hi," Frank said. "Can we ask you something?"

"Sure," Sandy replied. "As long as it's not for free food. You need tickets to buy."

"It's not that," said Joe. "We were just wondering if you saw a kid earlier. He's wearing a red long-sleeved shirt with a wide stripe on it and black high-tops."

Sandy stopped wiping and looked at him in surprise. "You know, I don't usually pay much attention to you younger kids," she said. "You all look alike to me. But I do remember him. I had to chase him away, like, three times to stop him from stealing all the napkins."

Frank glanced over at his brother. Stealing napkins? That sounded weird even for Adam. But it did mean that he'd been over at the snack bar just as he claimed.

"I guess Adam does have an alibi, after all,"

Joe said as Sandy hurried around behind the counter to wait on someone. "Let's go question Darryl again. Or maybe that Callie girl—I still think it's weird that she ran away earlier. Although I don't know if even Mimi would call her a prince. . . ."

Frank was staring at the napkin dispensers. There were two of them sitting at one end of the counter. They were big and made of shiny metal, with napkins sticking out the front through a large slot.

"Stealing napkins?" he mumbled. "Why would Adam do something like that? Unless . . ."

He raced over to the nearest dispenser and started pulling out the napkins. There were tons of them in there.

"What are you doing?" Joe said, sounding surprised.

"I have an idea." Frank kept yanking at the

napkins. Soon they were all out. He peered inside the dispenser. Nothing.

He stepped over to the second dispenser. By now Sandy had looked over and noticed what he was doing.

"Hey!" she yelled. "What's wrong with you twerps today? Stop messing with the napkins!"

Frank hesitated. He usually obeyed adults when they told him to do something—or *not* to do something. Besides, what if his theory was wrong? He would probably get in big trouble for wasting napkins.

But Joe had finally figured out what he was doing. "I'll check the other one!" he cried. He raced over and dumped the dispenser over. The napkins all came fluttering out.

So did a huge wad of cash!

10

Secret File #1: Solved!

"T hanks for the ride, Mom," Joe said as he and Frank climbed out of their mother's car. "Where's Dad? We want to tell him about the video game tournament."

That wasn't all they wanted to tell him about. During the whole ride home, Frank and Joe had kept quiet about the mystery they'd solved at Fun World that day. They wanted to tell their dad about it first.

Mrs. Hardy smiled. "I'm afraid that will have to wait. Your dad went to the home improvement store to pick up some more flooring for the spare room."

"Oh," Joe said. He and Frank traded a look. In all the excitement at Fun World, they'd almost forgotten about their secret bet. "Um, guess we'll go out and play in the woods, then."

"All right," his mother said. "But make sure you're back in time for dinner. Your dad is planning to grill some burgers tonight." She hurried toward the front door.

"I guess neither of us gets dibs on the spare room," Frank said as he and Joe headed around the side of the house. "After all, neither of us won the tournament."

Joe nodded. Adam had been kicked out of the video game tournament after Mr. Fun found out he'd stolen that money. When the contest had started up again, Iola had ended up winning first prize.

Frank had come in right after Iola, with Joe

trailing right behind Frank. Frank could practice all he wanted—but he'd forgotten that Iola won at almost everything.

Joe looked up at the spare room as they passed the garage. He really wanted that room. But he wasn't sure he should get it anymore.

"Maybe you should take the new room," he told Frank. "You were the one who figured out the answer to the mystery."

Frank shrugged. "Yeah. But I never could have done it if you hadn't caught up to Darryl on the bumper cars," he said.

That made Joe feel a little better. He thought about the case as he and Frank hurried across the yard and ducked into the woods.

"I still don't get it," he admitted. "I mean, I know Adam was the thief, since he confessed after we found the cash. But how'd you figure it out?"

Frank stepped ahead to pull down the ladder

for the tree house. "I'll tell you when we get up there."

Soon they were in the tree house. Frank left Joe to pull the ladder up by himself, and he went straight to the whiteboard and wrote down four names.

Joe turned around and saw the names. "Darryl,

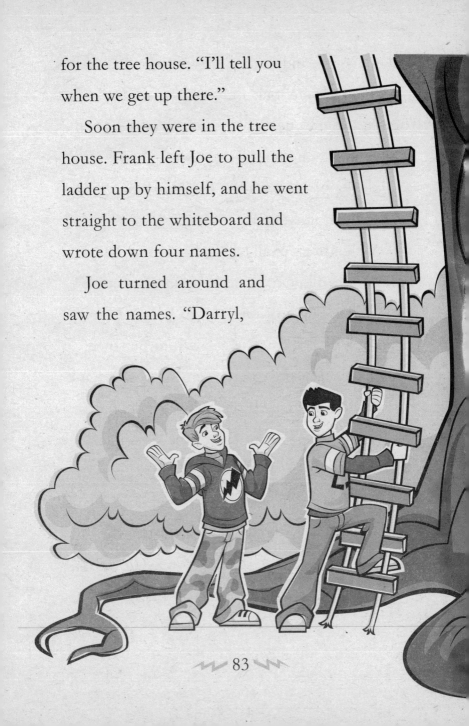

Adam, Mimi, and Callie," he read aloud.

"Those were our only real suspects," said Frank. "So the question was, which of them could have done it, and how?"

Joe flopped down on a floor cushion. "Okay. So what's the answer?"

"Well, after we talked to Mimi about her tickets, I remembered something kind of weird," Frank said. "Adam won a ton of tickets from his round of Blob Blaster. We saw him put them in his pocket. But they weren't in his pockets anymore when he emptied them out for Mr. Fun."

Joe gasped. "You're right!" he exclaimed. "I should have realized that too."

"I didn't really notice at first either," Frank admitted. "I only thought about it later when the Snack Shack lady said Adam was messing with the napkins. For a second I wondered if he'd stuck his tickets in there for some reason, but then I realized the truth."

"So Mimi spotted the cash on the floor after Darryl knocked it over," Joe said. "Just like we thought."

"Right. She must have picked it up, then been standing there in the hallway looking at it when Adam happened to walk past on his way to the Snack Shack," Frank said. "He tricked her into giving him the money and gave her his tickets as a 'reward.'"

"But why didn't Mimi just tell us that?" Joe wondered.

Frank rolled his eyes. "This is Mimi we're talking about, remember? She probably thought Adam was King of Pluto or something. Or maybe he was the one who told her he was a secret prince, and that she shouldn't give away his secret."

Joe laughed. "Okay. So then Adam knew everyone would suspect him right away, since he's bad news. . . ."

"Plus, he knew Mimi might tattle," Frank added. "And also that Callie saw him with the cash. So he hid it in the napkin dispenser, planning to come back for it later." He drew a circle around Adam's name on the dry-erase board. "But his plan didn't work."

"Busted!" Joe exclaimed. "Still, I'm not sure I ever would have figured it out."

"But you were the one who actually found the cash," Frank reminded him. "I was about to give up when the snack bar lady started yelling."

Joe laughed. "Maybe Dad's right. We do make a pretty good team."

"Just like Dad and his friends on the force." Frank held up his hand for a high five.

"Hardys rule!" Joe high-fived him back. "Hey, since we're such an awesome crime-fighting team, maybe we should look for more mysteries to solve."

Frank looked excited. "We could make the tree house our secret headquarters," he said. "We can take notes on the dry-erase board and help people all over Bayport."

"Sure," Joe said with a laugh. "But only if *you* take all the notes!"

Frank smiled. "It's a deal."

He wrote something else on the whiteboard. Joe leaned forward to read it, then grinned. It said:

IT'S A BEAUTIFUL DAY IN BAYPORT. . . .

Hey, Joe, what should we do today?

Nah. Did that yesterday.

Let's play zombies.

We could play catch.

Bo-ring!

I know what you boys can do today. Come with me.

WHERE WAS DAD TAKING THEM? FRANK AND JOE HAD NO IDEA. . . .

Why are we at the hardware store?

Just wait and see.

HARDWARE